Invasion of the Pig Sisters

Book #4

Story by Lisa Wheeler
Pictures by Frank Ansley

A Richard Jackson Book
Atheneum Books for Young Readers
New York London Toronto Sydney

Atheneum Books for Young Readers
An imprint of Simon & Schuster Children's Publishing Division
1230 Avenue of the Americas
New York, New York 10020
Text copyright © 2006 by Lisa Wheeler
Illustrations copyright © 2006 by Frank Ansley
Book design by Abelardo Martínez
The text of this book is set in Palatino.
The illustrations are rendered in ink and watercolor.
Manufactured in the United States of America
First Edition
2 4 6 8 10 9 7 5 3 1
Library of Congress Cataloging-in-Publication Data
Wheeler, Lisa, 1963–
Invasion of the pig sisters / Lisa Wheeler ; illustrated by Frank Ansley.— 1st ed.
p. cm. — (Fitch & Chip ; #4)
"A Richard Jackson Book."
Summary: When Fitch the wolf, who likes to have plans, and Chip the pig,
who likes surprises, decide to meet at the playground, their expectations
are tested by the presence of Chip's three little sisters.
ISBN-13: 978-0-689-84953-4 ISBN-10: 0-689-84953-2
[1. Friendship—Fiction. 2. Play—Fiction. 3. Surprise—Fiction.
4. Pigs—Fiction. 5. Wolves—Fiction.] I. Ansley, Frank, ill. II. Title
III. Series: Wheeler, Lisa, 1963– . Fitch & Chip; 4.
PZ7.W5657In 2005
[E]—dc22
2004003076

For my big sister, Gina,
and my little sister, Mary.
Love,
L. W.

For my wife, Pat.
—F. A.

Contents

1.

Plans

"Hooray!" squealed Chip.

"Tomorrow is Saturday!"

Chip turned cartwheels on the grass.

"Hooray for Saturday!" howled Fitch.

Fitch tried to turn a cartwheel.

He tripped over his tail.

"Let's meet at the park tomorrow,"

said Chip.

"When tomorrow?" asked Fitch.

"In the morning," said Chip.

"What time in the morning?"
  said Fitch. "I like to have a plan."

"Ten o'clock," said Chip.

"Good," said Fitch.

Fitch took out his notebook.

He took out his pencil. He wrote:
"Meet Chip at ten o'clock in the park."

"Where do you want to meet?"
  asked Fitch.

"At the playground," said Chip.

"Okay," said Fitch. He wrote it down.

"Meet Chip at ten o'clock in the park,

at the playground."

"What will we play?" asked Fitch.

"Anything we want," said Chip.

"I like to have a plan," said Fitch.

"I like to have surprises," said Chip.

Fitch sighed. His ears twitched.

"I know!" said Chip.

He turned another cartwheel.

"You can surprise me with your plan."

"I like that idea!" said Fitch.

"I will meet you tomorrow,"
said Chip.

"It's a plan!" Fitch said.

2.

Surprises

At ten o'clock on Saturday morning,

Fitch waited for Chip

at the park playground.

He waited . . .

and waited . . .

and waited.

He looked all around.

He hugged his tail.

Chip arrived at ten minutes
after ten o'clock.
He was not alone.
Three little pigs with ribbons
on their pigtails
stood behind him.

"You are late," said Fitch.

"Not *too* late," said Chip.

"You are not alone," said Fitch.

"I had to bring my little sisters,"
  said Chip.

"My mother went to market."

"Oh," said Fitch.

"What is the plan?" asked Chip.

Fitch let go of his tail.

He reached into his backpack.

He took out his list.

The three little pigs hid behind Chip.

"Why are they hiding?" asked Fitch.

"They have never met a wolf before," said Chip. "They are afraid."

"Afraid?" said Fitch.

"Afraid," said Chip.

"Of me?" asked Fitch.

"Of you," said Chip.

"I won't hurt a hair on their

chinny-chin-chins," said Fitch.

"I know that and you know that,"

said Chip.

"But they do not know that."

"Then I will show them," Fitch said.

He walked toward the three little pigs.

3.

Three Little Pigs

"Do not be afraid," said Fitch.

He smiled at the pig

with the yellow ribbon.

She covered her eyes.

"That is Honey," said Chip.

"She is afraid to see your big teeth."

Fitch covered his teeth with his paw.

"Is this better, Honey?"

Honey did not uncover her eyes.

"Hello," Fitch said to the pig

with the red ribbons.

She covered her ears.

"That is Suey," said Chip.

"She is afraid of your voice."

Fitch held his nose.

"How do I sound now?" he called.

Suey did not uncover her ears.

"What is *your* name?"

Fitch asked the pig

with the blue ribbons.

She covered her mouth.

"That is Bitsy," said Chip.

"She is afraid to talk to you."

"That is good, Bitsy," said Fitch.

"Little pigs should never talk
   to strangers."

Bitsy did not uncover her mouth.

The three little pigs stood very still.

Fitch stood very still too.

"I'm getting bored," said Chip.

"What is the plan?"

Fitch handed Chip a list.

It read:

PLANS FOR SATURDAY

4.

Change of Plans

Chip read Fitch's list.

PLANS FOR SATURDAY

1. Seesaw

"Come on," Chip called to Fitch.

"Let's ride the seesaw."

Fitch did not move.

"We cannot ride the seesaw,"

said Fitch. "Seesaws are for two."

"We *are* two," said Chip. "Me and you."

"We are five," said Fitch.

"Honey, Suey, Bitsy,

  plus you and me, make five."

Bitsy uncovered her mouth.

She smiled at Fitch.

Chip read the list again.

2. Swings

"We can all ride the swings!" said Chip.

"No, we cannot," said Fitch.

"There are four swings.

There are five of us.

That would not be fair."

Suey uncovered her ears.

She smiled up at Fitch
and listened closely.
Chip looked down
at Fitch's plan again.

3. Slide

"We can all play on the slide,"

said Chip.

"No, we cannot," said Fitch.

"Your sisters are too small

for that big slide.

It would not be safe."

Honey uncovered her eyes.

She looked at Fitch and smiled.

Then Suey spoke. "We can play

hide-and-seek."

"It is not in the plan!" said Chip.

"Then it is a surprise," said Fitch.

"You like surprises!"

5.

Fun for Five

"I *do* like surprises," said Chip.

"But playing with my sisters

is not a surprise."

"It is a surprise for me," said Fitch.

"But you like plans!" Chip said.

"Okay," said Fitch. "I plan to play

hide-and-seek with Honey, Suey,

and Bitsy."

Chip stomped his hoof.

He went off alone to cartwheel
on the grass.

The three little pigs moved
closer to Fitch.

Honey asked, "Do you have fangs?"

Suey asked, "Can you howl?"

Bitsy asked, "Where should I hide?"

First Fitch showed Honey his fangs.

Next he howled for Suey until
his throat was sore.

Then he showed Bitsy

the best places to hide.

"Now we are ready to play hide-and-seek," said Fitch. Chip turned cartwheels over to Fitch. "Can I play too?"

"Yes," said Fitch. "It is more fun with five."

"I will be IT," said Chip.

"You can jump out and surprise me."

"That sounds like a good plan,"
said Fitch.

Chip turned cartwheels
to the tree to be IT.

"Wait, Chip!" Fitch called.

"What about plan four?"

Chip pulled out Fitch's list.

4. Teach Fitch to cartwheel

"That is a good plan," said Chip.

"After hide-and-seek,

I will teach you *all* to cartwheel!"

Fitch smiled. "That will be fun for five!"

And it was.